river

MING'S ADVENTURE WITH
the Terracotta Army

This book is edited and designed by the Editorial Committee of *Cultural China* series

Story and Illustrations: Li Jian
Translation: Yijin Wert

Copy Editor: Susan Luu Xiang
Editor: Yang Xiaohe
Editorial Director: Zhang Yicong

Senior Consultants: Sun Yong, Wu Ying, Yang Xinci
Managing Director and Publisher: Wang Youbu

ISBN: 978-1-60220-983-1

Address any comments about *Ming's Adventure with the Terracotta Army* to:

Better Link Press
99 Park Ave
New York, NY 10016
USA

or

Shanghai Press and Publishing Development Company
F 7 Donghu Road, Shanghai, China (200031)
Email: comments_betterlinkpress@hotmail.com

Printed in China by Shenzhen Donnelley Printing Co., Ltd.

1 3 5 7 9 10 8 6 4 2

兵马俑

MING'S ADVENTURE WITH
the Terracotta Army

by Li Jian

Better Link Press

On his first visit to the museum, Ming became fascinated by the exhibition of the Terracotta Army of Qin Shihuang, who was the first emperor of China.

The life size terracotta warriors were buried in the Qin Shihuang Mausoleum in Shaanxi Province in northwest China.

The terracotta army was created to follow the first emperor of China into the afterlife.

Qin Shihuang ordered the construction of his mausoleum over 2,200 years ago. The building of the mausoleum lasted for 38 years and more than 700,000 people worked on it.

During his reign, Qin Shihuang standardized weights, measures, the written system of Chinese characters, and etc..

Map of the Qin Shihuang's mausoleum site

Xianyang Palace where Qin Shihuang lived

Qin Shihuang's army in his mausoleum

CHINA'S
TERRACOTTA
ARMY

To date, nine figures of generals have been found. Their front chests and shoulders are decorated with tassels, symbolizing their highest rank in the military.

All the Terracotta Army Generals are outfitted in ancient Chinese military officer caps adorned with tail-feathers of an ancient bird that is good at fighting, known as *he* (making the cap a *heguan*).

Ming was drawn to the Terracotta Army General. He looked very serious, calm and confident.

Ming's mother bought him a figurine of the General as a souvenir.

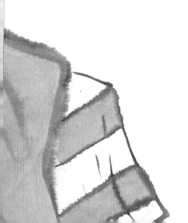

That night, Ming was suddenly awakened from his sleep by a loud noise. He saw some of his toys trying to take his Terracotta Army General figurine away.

"He's mine!" Ming screamed at them.

At that moment, the real Terracotta Army General pushed the door open and came to the rescue. He forced all the toys away!

The bronze chariot is 3.17 meters long and 1.062 meters high. It has 3,462 parts made of bronze, gold and silver. It is known as the best bronze relic in China.

The Terracotta said, "It will be a while before dawn. Do you want to go to a special place with me?"

"This is great!" Ming shouted happily when he saw a bronze chariot waiting in front of his home.

The four horses took off as if they were flying in the sky.

"Look! That's the mausoleum of Emperor Qin Shihuang where I live. It is a magnificent underground palace, but no one has ever seen all of it," the General said. "The Terracotta Army is only a small part of the mausoleum that guards this huge afterlife kingdom."

Pit 1

Pit 2

Pit 3

The structure of Qin Shihuang's mausoleum resembled the City of Xianyang, the capital of the Qin dynasty. The tomb consists of an interior city and an exterior city. The burial mound of the interior city has not been unearthed yet.

The terracotta army is located outside the exterior city. It has three pits with over 8,000 artifacts. Most were in fragments when they were unearthed. To date, over 1,000 pieces have been restored.

Interior City

Exterior City

Here is Pit 1. All the soldiers are outfitted in shorts with leather or cloth thigh protectors.

They landed shortly. "This is our base. These are my soldiers!" The General said.

"How huge the place is. Do you want to play hide and seek?" Ming asked.

"This should be interesting!" The General quickly hid behind a soldier.

"Be careful! Our weapons are very sharp!" An infantryman warned Ming.

"Is the General here?" Ming asked.

"No, he isn't." The infantryman said.

The Terracotta Army is made up largely of infantry. Their facial expressions vary from honest to attentive to longing to sadness. No two faces looked exactly the same. They are known as "the thousand faces with a thousand expressions". Some experts think that real soldiers served as models when the terracotta warriors were made.

Ming saw a terracotta warrior in light armor and said, "You are the General." He embraced him immediately. "I've got you now!"

"No! I am not a General," the terracotta warrior said. "I am a kneeling archer."

Pit 2 houses 332 archers who were positioned in combat formation.

Pit 2 revealed a well-equipped troop with 116 terracotta horses and a group of cavalryman standing in front of the horses.

"You are the General." Ming saw a terracotta warrior holding the reins of a horse. "I found you!"

"No, I am not a General. I am a cavalryman. The General may be at the headquarters. Try to look for him there," the cavalryman suggested.

The headquarters was in Pit 3, which was relatively small, but still Ming didn't find the General in there either.

The layout of Pit 3 is a concave covering about 520 square meters. Sixty-eight terracotta figurines, four chariot horses and a wooden chariot were found here.

Over thirty terracotta dancers were unearthed.
Most of them have naked upper bodies with
individualized facial characteristics.

"Perhaps the General went into the city!" Ming thought
as he walked towards the city wall. There, he met a group
of dancers.

"Have you seen the General?" Ming asked.

"I think he went over there to talk to the other
officers," one dancer told Ming.

Ming had to keep looking. Finally, he saw a General who looked like the General he was looking for.

"I found you!" Ming embraced him.

"You are wrong, I am not the General you are looking for. Although we wear similar caps, I am a civil official," the General look-alike said. "There is a garden nearby. Your General could be strolling in there. You should go there to look for him."

In ancient China, words were inscribed on wood or bamboo. Civil officials are outfitted in a knife and a knife-sharpener at their waist. These were so-called "pens" at that time.

Forty-six pieces of bronze birds, cranes, geese and swans were discovered. In Chinese culture, these animals symbolize longevity, luck and other good wishes.

Ming kept walking. By the river side, he met a terracotta farmer who was taking care of birds.

"Have you seen the General?" Ming asked.

"He hasn't been here. You should go back to where you were separated," the terracotta farmer said.

Over one hundred chariots were unearthed.

It was almost dawn, so Ming rushed back to where they had landed. There, he found the General standing in a chariot.

"I've finally found you!" Ming said excitedly.

"Please be quiet!" The General told him. "The Emperor will get angry if he hears a stranger. Let's go!"

"Where is the Emperor?" Ming asked curiously.

"That is a secret!" The General replied with a wink.

The bronze chariot with the four horses took off again.

At the blink of an eye, Ming was home.

"Thank you! I had a great night! I will visit you again in the museum," Ming said.

"You are welcome anytime!" The General replied.

Ming woke up the next morning and realized that he had dreamt of something magical. Looking at his souvenir, he felt the Terracotta Army General smiling at him.

Xi'an

Weihe River

Bahe River

Xi'an